Brown Bread
and Honey

Pamela Allen

Puffin Books

The King was the most important person in the land.
He lived in a big castle on top of a high hill.

With his friend the stable-boy he loved to jump,

he loved to run, and he loved to ride his horse.

But what he loved most of all was food.
All day, every day, in the castle kitchen,
the King's cooks cooked.

Stirring and whirring, mixing and fixing,
basting and tasting, sniffing and whiffing,

sipping and dipping, making and baking,
chopping and lopping, stewing and brewing.

Until at last they had made the King's dinner.

There were . . .

milkshakes and muffins,
puddings and pumpkins,
chicken and chocolate,
pavlova and pikelets,

curry and cordial,
lamingtons and liquorice,
custard and cake,
and more, and more, and more.

AND THE KING MANAGED TO EAT IT ALL.

But gradually,
little by little,
bit by bit,
he got slower and slower
and heavier and heavier,

until he was too slow to run,
too tired to jump,
and too heavy for his poor horse.

Nothing he did was any fun any more.

The King was miserable.
Nothing he ate tasted any good any more.
As each splendid new dish reached the table,
the King complained. He screwed up his face.
'This curry is too hot,' he cried.

'This gravy is too greasy,' he grizzled.
'These muffins are too mushy,' he moaned.
'This stuffing is too sticky,' he screeched.

The cooks were sad and they tried harder and harder
to make bigger and better dishes to please the King.

Then one evening after a big dinner

of pork pie, pease pudding and pavlova,

the King was sick.

VERY SICK.

He groaned and he moaned.
'OOOOOH! AAAAAH! OOOOOOH!'
Now he was SO miserable and SO tired
that he didn't want to see another pie,
pudding or pavlova, ever again.

He blamed the food. He blamed the cooks.
'It's all your fault,' he shouted. 'You're sacked!'
So the sacked cooks packed their bags
and went away.
Now there were no cooks left in the castle.

The next morning the King felt a little better
and wanted some breakfast.
He asked the maid who cleaned the kitchen,
'Can you cook?'
But the maid had heard him complaining about the curry.
So she said, 'No, I can't.'

Then he asked the gardener who grew the gardenias,
'Can you cook?'
But the gardener had heard him grizzling about the gravy.
So he said, 'No, I can't.'

Then he asked the minister in charge of the money,
'Can you cook?'
But the minister had heard him moaning about the muffins.
So he said, 'No, I can't.'

Then he asked the soldier who served as the sentry,
'Can you cook?'
But the soldier had heard him screeching about the stuffing.
So he said, 'No, I can't.'

When there was no one left to ask,
the King sat down just where he was and cried.
He was still sitting there the next day
when the stable-boy found him.

'Would you like some brown bread and honey,
Your Majesty?' asked the stable-boy,
holding out the lunch his mother had made.
Now the King had never tasted brown bread in his life.
He stopped crying. He looked at it carefully. He smelt it.
BUT HE DIDN'T COMPLAIN.
'Thank you,' he said in a tiny voice.

He took a bite.
'This is yummy!' he exclaimed in amazement,
and greedily gobbled up ALL of the lunch
and was looking around for more.

'There isn't any more,' said the stable-boy.
'That is all there is.'
'I'm sorry,' said the King in a tiny voice.
'But I was SO-O-O-O-O hungry.'

Each day from then on the stable-boy brought two lunches in two little boxes to the castle – one for the King and one for himself – and together they would sit under a shady tree to eat.

Until . . .   at last . . .

The King could jump, and run,

and ride his horse again.

This made the King very happy.

Now he loves messing about in the castle kitchen making meals with his friend the stable-boy.

And do you know what they like best of all?

BROWN BREAD AND HONEY.